Voyager

THE X FILES™

Hungry Ghosts

Novelization by Ellen Steiber

Based on the television series
The X-Files created by
Chris Carter

Based on the teleplay
written by Jeff Vlaming

HarperCollins*Publishers*

Voyager
An imprint of HarperCollins*Publishers*
77–85 Fulham Palace Road,
Hammersmith, London W6 8JB

This paperback edition 1998
9 8 7 6 5 4 3 2 1

First published in the USA by HarperTrophy
A division of HarperCollins*Publishers* 1998

Based on the episode 'Hell Money' by Jeff Vlaming

ISBN 0 00 648332 1

Set in Goudy

Printed and bound in Great Britain by
Caledonian International Book Manufacturing Ltd, Glasgow

My deep thanks to:
Barbara Drye, M.D., and
Charlie Goldberg, M.D., for
the medical consultation and
lunch in Chinatown; Mimi
Panitch for warning me about
the pitfalls; Rosa Schnyer for
Chinese medicine; and Sarah
Thompson for information on
China, its languages, and its
remarkable culture.

This book is for Sarah,
whose suggestions and help
were invaluable.

Chapter One

Although night had fallen, the streets of San Francisco's Chinatown were brightly lit. Most of the shops and restaurants were open despite the late hour, and locals and tourists crowded the narrow sidewalks. Chinatown was a city within a city where rooftops curved like ancient pagodas, brass dragons edged the streetlights, and neon business signs painted the night in both Chinese and English.

On this particular night, drums and cymbals clashed out an insistent rhythm, and sparklers burned like white-gold stars against the night.

A festival dragon was winding its way through the streets. The lead dancer held the great papier-mâché dragon head aloft in his hands: silver eyes, a massive forehead with a fringe of white beard, and a bright yellow collar. Behind him a serpentine line of dancers carried the long, blue-scaled body. As the drumbeat quickened, the head of the dragon whirled and reared up as though it might actually take flight.

While nearly everyone else was involved in the festivities, one young man obviously was not. He had more important matters on his mind as he hurried away from the crowds and the brightly lit streets.

It was a chilly September night, and the young man's breath rose in a fog in front of him. Despite the cool weather, he wore only a light zippered jacket over his shirt and jeans. He walked briskly, zigzagging through the main streets, passing the fruit vendors and markets and restaurants, and finally turning onto a smaller side street. He wouldn't allow himself to run. That would be panicking. That would make him obvious. Still, he couldn't help quickening his pace as he turned into a narrow alley.

A round of firecrackers went off a short distance behind him, and he jumped, covering his ears as though it had been gunfire. Whirling, he looked behind him to the front of the alley. Four teenagers stood there, laughing hysterically. Obviously, they'd set off the firecrackers. And he—he was as easily startled as a rabbit, he thought in disgust. Then again, tonight, he had a great deal in common with animals that were prey. He checked again. No, no one was following him. But he was too shaken to maintain his former semblance of calm. He turned and ran.

He drew back in terror as he nearly collided with a figure that stepped out from behind a fire escape. The figure towered over him, at least seven feet tall, with a long face and crossed eyes. The young man bit back a cry of alarm. Then he realized it was just one of the festival mimes—a man on stilts, his face covered by a mask.

The young man shouted angrily, then pushed the oversize mime out of his way and kept running.

3

He crossed the alley, then raced up the back stairs of a neglected brick building. The old wooden stairway creaked with each step. He was breathing hard, desperate to get off the streets, where he knew he was vulnerable.

He reached the landing and felt his racing heart slow. His breath began to come more easily. He was home. It was all right.

And then he saw that it wasn't all right.

Chinese lettering marked his door in shiny white paint. White, the color of mourning. As for the meaning of the lettering—he wouldn't even let himself believe that it might be true.

He reached out and touched the door, his hand trembling with trepidation. The paint was still damp, leaving white smudges across his fingertips. The freshness of the paint frightened him more than the message. Whoever painted it had been here recently.

Again he turned and looked behind him. Except for a stray dog, the alley was empty.

Slowly he opened the door to the apartment.

The inside was dark. The only light was the hazy glow of the streetlamps spilling in through the windows.

Moving silently, he stepped inside. Suddenly a flashlight switched on, its harsh white beam aimed directly into his eyes, blinding him, making it impossible to see the man who held it.

The stranger spoke to him in Cantonese, the language of their home. "You knew the rules. Now you pay the price."

"I told you I wanted out," the young man replied, raising his hand to shield his eyes.

"You start, you finish," the other answered.

The young man saw a metallic gleam. The man with the flashlight had drawn a knife.

But the young man had half expected this. A switchblade snapped open in his hand. In a quick strike, he slashed at the figure in front of him, cutting the man's chest and making him reel backward, dropping the light.

The young man caught his breath, wondering if he'd killed his attacker. His heart was pounding, his blood throbbing in his ears.

He'd never wanted to fight. And all he wanted now was to escape.

He took another ragged breath, then felt his body begin to shake violently. His attacker wasn't the only one in the apartment.

Three masked figures stood in the shadows. They wore long robes so black that they were nearly invisible in the darkened apartment. But their faces glowed with an unearthly white light. The young man had seen these faces before in old prints in his father's books. They were the faces of ancient Chinese demons. And now they had come for him.

The watchman sat frowning at the electronic blackjack game in his hand. He was in his late twenties, tall and strong, his head closely shaved. He wore the trademark white shirt, navy tie and side-striped pants of a rental security guard. He paid no real attention to the place where he was stationed, the Bayside Funeral Home. He deliberately ignored the open casket that sat at the front of the chapel just a few yards away from him. He didn't want to look at the body, at the three red paper lanterns hanging above the casket, or even at the flowers surrounding the coffin.

This was a new assignment for him. Earlier that day his younger brother had teased him about how creepy it would be to work in a funeral home. For a split second the guard let himself think about the stories his brother had told him: the one about the corpse that sat up in its coffin, crying out the name of its murderer; and another about a ghost who haunted morgues. Well, he wasn't about to let himself be spooked.

Suddenly, he heard a noise from another part of the funeral home. That was odd. He knew for certain that he was the only one there. He waited a moment, wondering if he'd imagined it. No, there it was again. A shuffling sound—almost as if something was being dragged across the floor.

His heart hammering, the guard turned the game off, stood up, and took out his long utility flashlight. Slowly he walked through the dark, empty chapel.

This was the first time since he had signed on with the security company that anything had happened on his shift; he could feel his adrenaline rising, his every sense heightened and alert.

As he moved into the arched hallway, suddenly there was another noise—as if something heavy was being moved or shut.

The watchman spun around and shined his flashlight along the walls of one of the receiving rooms. Nothing. He kept walking, beaming the light along the hallway and inside a room where sample coffins were displayed.

Then he went absolutely still as he heard a low rumbling. *No*, he told himself, *it couldn't be.* As he moved down the hallway to the source of the noise, he was sure he must be imagining things. Until he pushed open the painted red doors that led to the crematorium. His stomach started to churn as he realized he hadn't imagined the sound.

"Somebody in here?" he called out, his voice wavering as he pointed his flashlight in the direction of the lit oven.

Caught in his flashlight beam were three figures dressed in black robes, their faces painted white Chinese masks.

No sooner did his light catch them than they were gone—vanishing in the darkness. As if they'd never been.

Did I just imagine that? the watchman asked himself. He felt his entire body tense as he realized that his flashlight wasn't the only light in the room. There was a strange orange glow in the darkness. And a faint sound coming from within the crematorium, as if something—or someone—was inside.

It couldn't be.

"Holy Moses . . . ," he murmured softly, starting toward the oven. The sound grew louder. He moved faster, toward the circle of orange light. Then he leaned forward, peering through the glass spy hole in the oven door, dreading what he would see.

The crematorium was lit with the dancing orange light of fire. The watchman looked more closely, squinting against the glare of the flames. And what he saw made him sick.

A young Chinese man stared back at him, his face distorted with agony, his dying screams muffled by the thick oven wall and the roar of the flames.

Chapter Two

In the mortuary's embalming room, FBI Special Agent Dana Scully stood beneath the harsh light of an overhead fluorescent, staring down at the charred face of a young Chinese man. According to the police, the morgue's panicked security guard had turned off the gas jets as soon as he'd figured out how to work the controls. But unfortunately, he hadn't been fast enough. Even without a full autopsy, it was clear to Scully that it was the fires of the crematorium that had been the cause of death. Remnants of scorched and melted clothing still stuck to the corpse's blackened skin.

She looked down at the victim, then glanced at her partner, Fox Mulder. "What a way to go," she said, shaking her head.

Scully pulled on a pair of latex gloves and turned to Lieutenant Neary, the San Francisco plainclothes detective who'd accompanied them. Neary, a balding middle-aged man, looked as though he hadn't slept in days. Scully noted that he was keeping a careful distance between himself and the corpse. She wondered if he was just one of those people who were queasy around death, or if there was something about this particular body that disturbed him.

"You've seen this M.O. before, Detective?" Scully asked. "A man cremated alive?"

"Yeah," Neary replied uneasily. "Third time this year."

"The eleventh time, actually," Mulder said. "There were three in Seattle, three in Los Angeles, and two in Boston. All Chinese men between the ages of twenty and forty, all recent immigrants."

And that, Scully thought, was why she and Mulder were here. Fox Mulder was not the sort of FBI agent who pursued routine investigations. Mulder had a very particular area of interest, the investigation of what the FBI termed X-files, cases that dealt with the realm of the highly unusual and the paranormal. A string of deaths by such a bizarre method was exactly the sort of thing that piqued Mulder's interest.

The police lieutenant looked embarrassed by Mulder's knowledge. "We weren't able to determine the connection until just recently," Neary explained, sounding apologetic. "The other two bodies were much more badly burned. We got lucky with this one."

"Lucky," Mulder echoed as he gazed at the corpse. "That's an interesting word for it."

Scully began a cursory examination of the body; the autopsy would come later. Autopsies were routine for Scully, who had trained as a medical doctor and a physicist before joining the FBI. Years ago in medical school, she'd grown used to the gory, even to the grotesque. Blood didn't upset her. Neither did the natural decomposition of bodies.

But what she saw when she peeled back one of the victim's charred eyelids threw her.

Impossible, she told herself. *The victim was burned too severely for this to be physically possible.* A dark brown eye, unharmed by the fire, stared back at her.

She peeled back the reddened, blistered lid even farther. Using a tongue depressor, she gingerly touched the eyeball. She released a sigh of relief as she realized: The eye was made of glass.

Mulder and Scully followed Neary to the funeral home crematorium to have a look at the site of the death. Other detectives were still on the scene. One was dusting for prints. Another was taking a formal statement from the owner of the funeral home.

"The night watchman says he saw three men in here right before he found the victim," Neary reported. "He says the three men were all wearing some sort of mask—like Chinese face paint."

Mulder peered inside the long, narrow oven. Its floor was covered in fine gray ash.

"You have any leads on this case, Detective?" he asked. "Any thoughts or ideas?"

Neary shrugged. "These last few years, we got a big influx of immigrants from Hong Kong. People who wanted to get out before Hong Kong returned to Chinese control."

That didn't surprise Mulder. For well over a hundred years now, Chinese immigrants had been streaming into the United States. The recent wave of immigration that Neary was referring to had its roots in 1898. That was the year that China, then a monarchy, signed a treaty with the British, leasing Hong Kong to them for ninety-nine years. In the time that followed, the Chinese government had changed, becoming the People's Republic of China. Although the rest of the country was under Communist rule, the People's Republic had honored the old treaty, and British-ruled Hong Kong had become a thriving international port. Mulder knew that in the last decade, thousands of Hong Kong's residents had fled China, fearing what life might be like when the Communist government took over on July 1, 1997, the date the treaty expired. Many of those immigrants wound up in American port cities: New York, San Francisco, Boston, and Seattle.

"A lot of the Chinese immigrants are legal," Neary went on. "And a lot of them aren't. In any case, we've got over thirty thousand people packed together in a relatively small area. Many of them aren't fluent in English, so finding any job that isn't a dead end is a struggle. Getting a decent apartment is next to impossible. You wouldn't believe how many gave up everything they had just to get out of China. Which means serious poverty. A lot of these people are flat-out desperate."

"Those are exactly the kinds of conditions that result in stepped-up gang activity in any community," Scully said.

Neary nodded. "Chinatown's no different. But so far we can't tie these deaths to anyone or anything."

Mulder leaned into the oven, bending backward to examine its ceiling. He didn't really expect to find anything there, but he'd learned long ago not to overlook any detail.

His eyes widened and he stood up again, intrigued by what he'd found. He turned to Neary. "You got anybody that can read or speak Chinese?"

"Yeah, Glen Chao," Neary answered. "He's right over there. Why?"

"Will you get him?" Mulder asked. He showed Neary what he'd seen: Scratched with soot on the ceiling of the oven was a Chinese character. "I want to see if he can read this for me."

"Sure," Neary said. He gestured to one of the other detectives, and a clean-cut, good-looking young man, wearing a police badge on his suit, stepped forward.

Neary made the introduction: "Glen Chao, Agent Mulder."

"Hi," Chao said. "What have you got?"

Although he was obviously of Chinese descent, Chao spoke English without a trace of an accent.

Mulder shined his light on the character again. "There's something written up here on the ceiling," he told Chao. "I was wondering if you could read it."

Chao leaned in. "Yeah," he said, his voice soft with surprise.

"I'd like to know what it says," Mulder told him.

"It says *gui*. It means 'ghost.'"

"Ghost?" Mulder echoed.

"Does that mean anything to you?" Neary asked the FBI agent.

"Well, I don't know," Mulder said thoughtfully. "But it's a strange thing for a man being burned alive to write, don't you think?"

"Think it could be connected to those three guys in masks?" Neary asked.

"Maybe," Mulder said. Once again he scanned the inside of the oven. He leaned in farther, staring at the back corner of the crematorium, an area not directly exposed to the flames. There in the ashes he found a small triangle of printed paper. He drew it out and held it up for closer inspection.

"What's this?" he asked. "Anybody recognize this? It looks like some kind of foreign currency."

Chao spoke up. "It's called 'hell money.' It's used as an offering at burials and during the Chinese Festival of the Hungry Ghosts."

Mulder fingered the bit of paper. "Is it worth anything?" he asked, trying to understand.

"It's not money, per se," Chao explained. "It's a symbolic offering to evil spirits and the ghosts. For good luck and to keep the spirits pacified."

"Pacified?" Neary echoed.

"You know how the ancient Egyptians used to bury their dead with all the precious objects they'd need in the afterlife?" Chao said. "Well, Chinese burials were very similar. In the early dynasties, kings and queens had their servants killed to accompany them to the afterworld. Later on, they began to use models instead. Back in the third century B.C., the First Emperor's grave included an entire life-size pottery army. Hell money is a leftover from those times. You send money with the dead so that they'll have what they need in the afterlife and so that their angry ghosts won't come back and cause trouble for you."

Mulder exchanged a glance with Neary. "Where would I get this hell money?"

"You'd have it printed for yourself in Chinatown," Chao answered.

Mulder handed the small triangle of paper to Chao. "Maybe we just found a way to identify the body," he said.

Chapter Three

"The victim's name was Johnny Lo," Scully said the next morning, looking at the notes she'd gotten from Detective Neary's unit.

She stopped reading for a moment and looked around her. She and Mulder were in a narrow alley edged with tall brick buildings. While just a few blocks away the main streets of Chinatown were bustling with the morning's business, this alley was quiet, shut down. Discarded packing cartons and open trash cans were piled against the buildings. Shiny red firecracker casings littered the ground. These buildings were supposed to be industrial, Scully guessed—warehouses and factories. But judging from the drawn blinds on the windows of the upper floors, it seemed that they'd become apartments, with their tenants trying to shut out the sights, sounds, and smells of the city below.

Scully glanced again at her notes and continued with what she'd found out. "He came here six months ago from Canton."

"Legally?" Mulder asked.

"Yes," Scully replied. "He was still in the INS application process. He worked as a dishwasher in one of the restaurants here."

"How many dishes do you have to break before your boss tosses you in an oven?" Mulder wondered aloud.

"I think it's pretty clear this is some kind of horrific cult or gang retribution killing," Scully said.

Mulder asked the question that had been troubling him since the previous night. "Well, why would the victim write the character for *ghost* on the inside of the crematory oven?"

"I don't know," Scully admitted.

"The guard described three figures. He said they seemed to vanish without a trace."

"So now you think we're chasing ghosts?" Scully asked.

"'Who ya gonna call?'" Mulder joked, quoting the *Ghostbusters* slogan.

When Scully didn't respond, Mulder continued.

"Ghosts or ancestral spirits have been central to Chinese spiritual life for centuries," he said quite seriously. "Chao is right. The Chinese believe that if you don't honor your ancestors properly, they become angry ghosts who haunt you. All sorts of misfortune and bad luck are attributed to the enraged spirits of ancestors."

Scully didn't even bother to conceal her skepticism. "You're saying that ancestral spirits pushed Johnny Lo into the oven and turned on the gas?"

"Well, it gives a new meaning to respecting your elders, doesn't it?" Mulder asked, teasing her again.

Scully sighed. She really wouldn't be surprised if Mulder did think that ghosts were responsible for the victim's death. Mulder was probably the only agent in the history of the FBI who had a poster in his office that read,

"I Want To Believe." And in the time they'd worked together, he'd asked her to believe in much stranger theories.

They climbed a steep flight of wooden stairs to Johnny Lo's apartment. The door was ajar. Glen Chao stood in front of it, waiting for them.

"I checked all the neighboring buildings," Chao reported. "Nobody saw or heard a thing. Not surprisingly. The festival was going on last night. Most people were on the streets, watching the dragon dance. All anybody heard was drums and firecrackers."

Mulder pointed to the broad white strokes of the Chinese characters painted on Johnny Lo's door. "What does this say?" he asked.

"I don't recognize it," Chao answered. "It could be—uh—idiomatic. Some kind of code."

Scully touched the paint with her fingers. "It's still tacky," she said. "Someone painted this very recently."

Mulder turned to Chao. "Could you copy this down for me?" he asked.

"Yeah, sure." Chao took out a notepad and began to copy the characters as the two FBI agents stepped into the apartment.

"Talk about tacky . . ." Mulder murmured.

Johnny Lo hadn't had much money. The apartment was furnished with the kind of cheap, beat-up furniture found in junk shops. Yellowed wallpaper peeled off the walls. A sheet of dusty plastic had been taped over a broken window, and the doors on the kitchen cupboards were warped by age and dampness.

Mulder moved to the cupboards and opened them. They were bare, as was the inside of the refrigerator.

Scully examined the surface of a Formica table. The thick layer of dust on top outlined a clean circle and a clean square.

"Look at this," she said, pointing to the table. "Someone's been here. This place has been cleared out."

Mulder sniffed the air. "What's that smell?"

"Maybe it's this new carpet," Scully said.

"Yeah. That's what it looks like," Chao

agreed, not seeming to find it very important.

Mulder, however, looked down at the spotless carpet and suddenly realized how different it was from everything else in the room. There was no way Johnny Lo could have afforded brand-new carpeting. Scully's thoughts were following a similar track. "What slumlord would spring for new carpet in a dump like this?" she asked.

Mulder walked over to the corner of the room and pulled up the edge of the carpeting. "Looks like they saved some money on carpet tacks and didn't even bother to replace the old padding," he said.

Scully continued checking out the apartment. She moved past Chao into an alcove, opening the drawers of a small desk. She found nothing until she came to a drawer containing several white paper packets with red Chinese writing on top of them. She held them up. "What's this?"

"Chinese herbal medicine," Chao answered.

"And what about this?" She held out a

bowl that contained something small and dried and brown.

Chao turned it over with his pen. "That's a dried frog," he said. "I think they're sometimes used as charms. For good health and prosperity—a protection."

"Looks like Mr. Lo could have used a little of both," Mulder said in a grim tone. Still kneeling by the edge of the rug, he pulled back the carpeting and revealed a dark bloodstain on the old padding. "Let's get this blood tested," he said.

"You think that blood is Johnny Lo's?" Chao asked.

Mulder nodded and stood up. "Either his or his murderer's."

Chapter Four

His long workday over, Shuyang Hsin entered his apartment and set a package wrapped in white paper on the kitchen table. As he did every evening, he took off his jacket and hung it on a hook in the living room. The logo on the back of his jacket read BAY AREA CARPETEERS.

Hsin was in his forties, a slight man with short black hair and kind, alert eyes. Using the spare, practiced motions of someone who knows how to move gracefully in small spaces, he returned to the kitchen, filled a metal tea-kettle with water, and lit the stove's gas flame. Night made the apartment seem even smaller than it was. When evening fell the rooms seemed to draw into themselves, cloaked in shadows that even the lamps couldn't entirely dispel. The apartment was not a cheerful place, Hsin reflected, especially for someone who couldn't leave it.

He unwrapped the white package, taking out two fried bean-paste balls. Carefully he cut the top of each one with a pair of scissors, then arranged them on a plate. He set the plate and a well-used porcelain teapot on a tray and carried them into the larger of the apartment's two narrow bedrooms.

Hsin's seventeen-year-old daughter, Kim, lay on the bed in a light sleep. By the soft light of a bedside lamp Hsin watched her, looking in vain for a sign that she was better. He was too honest to fool himself. Today was the same as yesterday and the day before. Kim's eyes had dark circles beneath them. Her face was pale and drawn. And she was so thin, wasting away. It seemed that every day a little bit more of her vanished.

He sat down beside her and poured a cup of tea. Kim's eyes opened. She gave him a weak smile, then raised herself against the pillows.

"What did you buy?" she asked, nodding toward the plate. Although Kim could speak both English and Chinese, she knew Chinese was easier for her father and always used it when they spoke.

"It's for you," Hsin answered, setting the tray on her lap. "Eat," he urged her.

She pushed a strand of long black hair back away from her face, looping it behind her ear. The sight of the food made her queasy. It had been well over a month since she'd had any appetite. Still, she wanted to please her father. And she realized it had been a while since they'd really talked.

"Stay and have tea with me," she said.

Her father didn't meet her eyes. "I have to go out."

"Where?"

"To see someone."

"Always seeing people," Kim murmured. "What kind of people?"

"I have business," her father said. "To make money. So you can get well."

"You can go tomorrow," Kim said. She knew she shouldn't argue, and she didn't mean to be disrespectful, but she found it odd that her father was always going to mysterious meetings that he'd never discuss with her.

"Money can pay for doctors," her father reminded her.

"No meeting is going to bring us that much money," Kim told him wearily. "The doctors said the procedure costs thousands."

Her father got to his feet. "Don't talk like that! Not ever!" he snapped. Before she could apologize, he left the room, closing the door behind him.

Leaving Kim alone again. That was the worst part of being sick, she thought, even worse than the weakness and pain. Being sick meant she stayed alone for hours in the tiny, dark apartment, never seeing or talking to anyone except her father. Being so alone scared her more than the disease itself. It made her feel as though everyone were deserting her, as though she were being left to die.

In one of Chinatown's dark alleys, a single lightbulb lit a sign over a doorway that read, PRIVATE: RESTAURANT DELIVERIES. Hsin went up to the door and knocked loudly.

After a moment a tall man answered the door, opening it just a crack. The two men exchanged a short, clipped conversation before the door opened wider and Hsin was admitted.

Hsin's chest tightened with a familiar fear as he walked through the restaurant and climbed the long, narrow stairway that led to the second floor.

Hsin's steps faltered as he entered the gaming room. Walking in was always hard, and yet he had to do it. Long ago, he'd committed himself to returning again and again. Until he won.

As always, thick cigarette smoke rose to the ceiling of the dim, crowded room. It was all men in here. Men sitting at tables or on rows of folding chairs, all of them speaking

Chinese. Like Hsin, most of them were working class, wearing jackets and work shirts. And like Hsin, all of them felt the tension in the room.

The crowd suddenly quieted as a door at the front of the room opened and three men in well-tailored suits entered. The first, a distinguished-looking man with a handsome but hard face, was empty-handed. The second man, Mr. Lau, was balding and wore gold wire-rimmed glasses. He was carrying two pale-green jade vases, one small, the other quite large. The third man, Mr. Wong, had a gray beard and held a hand-carved wooden box. In a solemn procession, they walked through the crowd to a polished teak table that sat on a raised platform at the front of the room.

With deliberate, practiced motions, Lau set the small vase down on the table and gave the larger one to the man who'd led the procession. His name was Mr. Tam, Hsin remembered.

Tam began to circulate the large vase through the room. He watched carefully as each man placed a tile inside the vase, then passed it to the man next to him. Hsin glanced at the tile he held in his hand, wondering if tonight it would bring him luck.

At the teak table, Wong opened the lid of the wooden box and held it high. A hum of excitement went through the room like a vibrating wire. The box was filled with thick stacks of hundred-dollar bills.

The man beside Hsin nodded and pointed to the box, but Hsin's eyes were on the large jade vase. It was rapidly making its way toward him. Shouts of encouragement echoed as each man placed the tile bearing his name in the vase.

Finally the jade vase came around to Hsin. Slowly, almost reverently, he dropped his tile into the vase, heard it clink against the jade.

Hsin's eyes went to the teak table, where Lau was polishing triangular tiles with a dark brown cloth. One by one, he'd polish a tile and then drop it into the small jade vase. A red tile, then another red tile, each vanishing inside the translucent walls of jade. Finally he picked up a white tile edged with wood. He rubbed it with the cloth, then set it aside.

Tam brought the large jade vase back to the table. A hush fell over the room as Lau stood up and reached inside the larger vase. Hsin felt himself start to sweat as Lau stirred the tiles with his hand, then slowly drew one out.

He read the name on it aloud: *"Li Oi-Huan!"*

The silence in the room broke, and Hsin shut his eyes in anxiety and relief.

Lau lifted up the small jade vase. The cries in the room rose as he held the white tile high, then dropped it into the vase.

Now the smaller vase was passed from hand to hand.

Until it found its destination in the hands of a wiry man in a light tan jacket. Hsin had noticed him earlier. Li had one milky eye and had looked terrified from the start.

Now Li's hands shook as he held the vase high overhead and shook it twice. The shouts of encouragement dropped to a hush as Li reached into the vase and his hand closed on one of the tiles.

He drew out a red tile and read it quickly, a stricken expression crossing his face. He clasped his fist tightly around the tile.

Mr. Tam was at Li's side at once. Gently he pried open the wiry man's fist, took the tile from his hand, and read it aloud. "*Xin!*"

The word sent the room into a din. Men were on their feet instantly as Mr. Tam took Li by the arm and escorted him firmly from his seat.

The two men who sat at the teak table were expressionless as Li was led through the door at the front of the room and it shut behind him.

Mr. Wong stroked his beard and stood up. Solemnly he shut the carved wooden chest. Beside him Mr. Lau lifted the two jade vases. Then they, too, left the room, exiting by the same door that Li had gone through.

Hsin watched for a moment as the men around him sat back in their chairs and raised their glasses in relief. Then he stood and hurried out of the room.

The game was over. At least for this night.

Chapter Five

Scully stared into one of the large jars in the glass case. It was filled with a clear liquid, in which was floating something that looked like a large root. She moved on to the next jar. It, too, held an unidentifiable organic object.

"I couldn't tell you what any one of these things is," she said to Mulder and Chao.

The three officers were paying a late visit to one of the many apothecaries that lined the streets of Chinatown. The name of this particular one was printed on the packets Scully had found in Johnny Lo's apartment.

"Well, they're roots mostly," Chao explained. "Ginseng, turmeric, astragalus, ephedra. Then you've got your more exotic stuff. Bear gallbladder, snake, shark fin . . . usually the doctor prescribes a mixture of herbs and then the patient brews it in a tea."

"So what was the victim using?" Mulder asked.

Glen Chao put the packages of dried herbs they had found in Johnny Lo's apartment on the counter. The pharmacist was busy weighing a finely sliced root in an old-fashioned brass hand scale. An abacus sat on the counter beside her. After weighing the root, she did a quick calculation, then added what looked like dried mushrooms to the scale. She was a middle-aged woman, wearing a dress with a high mandarin collar and a necklace of bright red beads. Intent on her work, she seemed unaware of the three officers.

She looked up only when Chao asked her what the herbs were. She opened the packets, glanced inside, and answered in rapid Cantonese.

"She says it's skullcap root and Chinese angelica," Chao explained to the two FBI agents. "They're used as painkillers."

"For what kind of pain?" Scully asked.

"Headaches and toothaches, mostly," Chao answered.

"Does she remember Johnny Lo?" Scully asked. "Or remember selling them to him?"

Chao translated the question. The pharmacist nodded.

"Ask her if she knows he's dead," Mulder said.

Chao did as Mulder asked, and the woman shook her head.

"Ask her if she recognizes those characters that were painted on his door," Mulder said.

Chao took out his notepad and held it up so that the pharmacist could read the symbol he'd copied. For the first time the woman's expression became alarmed. She answered Chao's question in staccato Chinese, then walked away from them, putting an end to the interview.

"What was that about?" Scully asked, puzzled.

"She says the house was branded a *tsang fang*—a haunted house," Chao replied.

"Haunted," Mulder repeated. "You mean by ghosts?"

Chao nodded. "Yeah. It's hard to give an exact translation, but it's what I was telling you about before—what the Chinese call *Yu Lan Hui*. The Festival of the Hungry Ghosts."

"The same festival they print the hell money for," Mulder said.

Chao continued with his explanation. "You see, on the fifteenth day of the seventh moon in the Chinese calendar, it's believed the gates of hell are opened and the ghosts of unwanted souls roam the earth, only returning on the last day of the month.

"It is believed that after death one is reborn into one of six worlds," Chao went on. "The worst of these worlds is hell. After that is the realm of the hungry ghosts—spirits who are condemned to eternal hunger and thirst. They are always starving and parched. They wander in continual torment, able to see water but unable to swallow it. Restless and plagued with desire, they often turn against the living.

"During *Yu Lan Hui* believers protect themselves by leaving gifts of food and hell money outside their homes to appease the ghosts—to keep them from coming inside and causing trouble. It is the only time that the appetite of the hungry ghosts can be appeased."

"The festival sounds similar to others," Mulder said thoughtfully. "The Japanese O-Ban, the Celtic Samhain, the Mexican Day of the Dead. All of them celebrate a time when the veil between the world of the living and the world of the dead dissolves and the dead return to roam the earth. And in each culture, the living make offerings to the dead."

"I don't know about the Celts," Chao said, "but both the Japanese and the Mexicans have a much friendlier relationship with their dead than the Chinese do. In their festivals you're meant to dance with the dead. The Festival of the Hungry Ghosts is much darker. Our offerings to the dead aren't always enough."

"What do you mean?" Scully asked.

"For some spirits, the ghosts most feared by our people, there's no buying them off: the

Preta, the ancient ghost of a murdered man who wanders the earth, exacting his revenge on the living. Or the *Wu Chang Kuei*, who collects the souls of doomed men and drags them down to *Ti Yu*," Chao continued, "to the Chinese Hell."

"So," Mulder said, trying to apply Chao's explanation to the case, "Johnny Lo didn't have enough hell money or enough of an offering, and the ghosts came for him. Is that what you're trying to tell us?"

Chao shrugged as they left the pharmacy. "I'm a cop. I don't usually name ghosts as suspects."

"But you think this murder could be related to *Yu Lan Hui*?" Mulder pressed.

"Well, it makes a strange kind of sense," Chao said. "This year's festival has just been completed."

"How about you, Detective?" Scully asked. "Do you believe in *Yu Lan Hui*?"

Chao smiled for the first time, though it was an ironic smile.

"I find it hard to argue with more than two

thousand years of Chinese belief—the things my parents and grandparents believe in. But the truth is," he added, "I'm more haunted by the size of my mortgage payments."

Oi-Huan Li sat in a hard-backed chair in a dark, hazy room. He was drinking from a small porcelain cup. He held it with both hands, trying to stop himself from trembling as he swallowed the hot liquid. It had a bitter taste, and though the drink was warm it made him feel cold inside. He had sat in this same chair before. This time, though, was different. He had never felt so frightened, so completely alone.

And then he realized he was no longer alone.

An ancient man materialized out of the gloom. He appeared translucent, though the robe he wore was from a century past. And behind him stood another ancestor. Older. Frailer. And even more ghostly . . .

Li's trembling ceased as the tea began to take effect. Another ghostly figure—an old woman in pauper's rags—materialized, followed by a third and fourth. . . .

The ancient ghostly man approached Li, reaching toward him. Mesmerized, Li stared at the ghost's hand with his one good eye. The skin was wrinkled and papery. The spectral hand came closer and closer.

Until it touched Li's chest and then disappeared.

Li felt ice inside his chest. And then a sudden agonizing pain.

The ancestor's hand suddenly drew back— as though it had taken something from him. Li's good eye widened, unable to believe what he saw. In the spectral hand was a human heart. A bloody, still beating human heart.

Li tried to reach for his chest, but the drug had taken hold. He couldn't move his hand at all. His eyes closed and his body went limp.

A man wearing white surgical gloves entered the room and took the empty cup from him. The man lifted Li's chin, pulled open an eyelid, stared at Li's dilated pupil, and nodded.

Chapter Six

Midnight was an eerie, quiet time at Highland Park Cemetery. The fog was in from the Bay, making the cool, damp night so dark it seemed opaque. A patrolman's truck moved along the access road inside the cemetery, its lights washing across the headstones and markers.

The patrolman slowed as his headlights illuminated a steep pile of dirt flanking an open grave—and something moving in the light.

Wait a minute, he thought, hitting the brakes. As far as he knew, he was the only one who was supposed to be here at this time of night. The gravediggers and administrative personnel went home well before dark. Even the caretaker had gone home.

The patrolman stared out at the scene illuminated by the glare of the headlights. He felt his blood run cold in his veins. Two figures stood by the side of the open grave. They stood as still as statues. As if, like the statues in the cemetery, they'd been there for generations.

As if they were waiting for him.

Each figure's body was covered by a long black robe. And where there should have been faces, there were painted white masks, each a grotesque demon.

The patrolman felt his heart begin to pound as a third masked figure rose slowly from the depths of the open grave.

Fighting down his fear, he told himself it had to be a prank. Bored teenagers hanging out at a cemetery on some kind of crazy dare. Well, they wouldn't think it was such a cool idea when he was done with them. Angry now, he got out of the truck. "Hey!" he shouted. "What are you doing?"

Holding his flashlight in front of him, the watchman started toward the figures.

But just as suddenly as they had appeared, they were gone. Swallowed by the darkness.

As if by magic.

Mulder barely heard the knock on the door of his hotel room. He was sitting at the desk, concentrating on the screen of his laptop. "What?" he asked.

"Mulder, you still awake?" Scully called.

Almost reluctantly, he got up and opened the door. "What's up?" he asked.

"I don't know how helpful this will be," Scully said, "but I called an old colleague, a neurologist who studied in China and incorporates Chinese medicine in her practice. She just got back to me a few minutes ago. Seems it's a very complex system. What she explained to me was that the ancient Chinese saw each human as a mini-ecosystem of sorts. They believed that the forces that work on the earth—like wind, heat, and moisture—also work on us. According to Chinese medicine, everything in the human body and psyche corresponds to the elements, the seasons, and their energies.

"For example, if someone is suffering from bronchitis, the Chinese physician would not only see it as an inflammation of the bronchi, but as connected to grief, to cold, and to an imbalance of the element metal. The goal of treatment by a Chinese practitioner is to prevent sickness by balancing the elements and energies in the body."

Mulder grinned at her. "Do I detect a note of skepticism?"

Scully shrugged. "Acupuncture has been proven effective in treating pain and addictions. And the neurologist I spoke with is first-rate. She wouldn't be using Chinese medicine in her practice if she wasn't seeing empirical proof that it worked. She did tell me, though, that she's run into one problem treating patients who hold to the traditional beliefs in ancestors and their spirits."

"What's that?" Mulder asked.

"Several of her elderly Chinese patients

refused necessary surgery. They say that the body is a gift from the ancestors, and therefore to cut it up or remove part of it dishonors the ancestors' spirits." Scully leaned against the wall, suddenly looking tired. "None of this tells us a whole lot about Johnny Lo's death."

"No, but it may be useful. Actually"— Mulder took off his glasses and rubbed his eyes—"I have no idea of what will be useful on this case. I was just doing more research. Did you know that in Chinese the word for 'ghost' and the word for 'demon' are the same, and those hungry ghosts that Chao described are supposed to hang out around graveyards and—"

Scully's cell phone cut off Mulder's words. "Scully here," she said, after flipping it open.

She listened for a few seconds then turned back to Mulder. "That was Neary," she said. "He asked us to meet him at Highland Park Cemetery."

Mulder and Scully found the cemetery lit by the flashing red and blue lights of police cars.

Glen Chao, they saw, had parked a few feet away and was just getting out of his car.

Lieutenant Neary greeted them with a curt nod, then led them through the tombstones.

"A night patrolman described three men wearing the same masks as the ones ID'd at the crematorium," he explained.

"What were they doing here?" Scully asked.

"We don't know exactly," Neary admitted. "They were spotted around this open grave over here, but we can't figure out exactly what they were up to."

"Is this a newly dug plot?" Mulder asked, looking at the pile of freshly turned dirt.

"Yeah," Neary answered. "They've got a burial service here at noon tomorrow."

"Chinese?" Mulder guessed.

"I don't know," Neary said. "We can check. Hey, Chao"—he gestured to the detective— "see if you can get the name of the future occupant."

Scully frowned. "I still don't see what anyone would want with an empty grave," she said.

Both Scully and Chao watched in puzzlement as Mulder, without warning, jumped into the hole.

"What the hell is he doing?" Neary asked, shining his flashlight into the grave.

"Something just occurred to me," Mulder said, concentrating on the damp earth beneath his feet.

He knelt and dug down a few inches, then stopped as he felt something beneath his fingertips. Something cold and smooth, almost rubbery.

He forced himself to keep digging. Until he had brushed away some of the dirt that covered the human face.

"What did you find?" Scully called down.

Mulder continued his grim task until he had revealed the face of a thin Chinese man.

This time, he thought, *they didn't bother with the crematorium.*

"Mulder?" Scully said.

Mulder's answer was terse. "Looks like there were going to be two burials tomorrow."

Chapter Seven

It was almost three A.M. when Scully and Mulder arrived at the coroner's office in the Central Police Station. Scully was exhausted. Yet she was the one who'd decided this couldn't wait, who'd requested that the body they'd found in the open grave be brought here straightaway.

She tied back her hair, put on a white medical coat and latex gloves, then entered the autopsy room. They were all alike, she thought wearily. The wall of refrigerated metal drawers, each storing a cadaver. Other corpses were laid out on metal gurneys, covered by a thick layer of translucent plastic. The sterile, gleaming metal counters, the glass cabinets containing the scalpels, syringes, and forceps. Harsh fluorescent lights and the smells of alcohol and disinfectant. Rooms designed for the examination of the dead. She thought briefly of what Chao had told them. What, she wondered, would a culture that believed in the afterlife make of this place?

Scully began making silent notes to herself before beginning her official examination of the body. The young man's clothing had been removed, but there was still dirt from the grave on his exposed skin. He was in his late twenties, and from what Scully could tell, his life hadn't been an easy one.

She didn't like what she'd seen so far. Among the hundreds of autopsies she'd performed, this was one of the most disturbing.

She looked up as Mulder walked in. "What did you find?" he asked.

"A lot," Scully said in a bleak voice. "And I haven't even finished my preliminary visual exam. Look at this."

She pulled back the plastic sheet that covered the body. The young man's face was bruised, and his thin torso was crisscrossed with scars—fine red lines creasing the pale flesh. Most noticeable, however, was a ropy incision running down the sternum, still stitched with catgut.

"This guy's body looks like a jigsaw puzzle," Scully told Mulder. "These are all surgical incisions. And judging by the color of the scars, I'd say they were all made within the last year."

"What was wrong with him?" Mulder asked.

"If you ask me," Scully replied, "nothing."

"Nothing? What do you mean?"

"Do you know what the human body is worth, Mulder?" she asked.

"Depends on the body," Mulder joked. Then he became serious as he saw her expression. "I don't know . . . a few bucks. . . . How much?"

"It's worth a fortune," Scully told him.

"You're saying that this guy was selling his body parts for money?"

Scully pointed to various scars on the corpse. "A kidney, a portion of the liver, a cornea, bone marrow . . . a person can lose these things and still live to cash his Social Security checks."

"He won't be cashing any Social Security checks anytime soon," Mulder said.

"No," Scully agreed, putting on a pair of plastic goggles. "But if I'm right, this is one man who truly left his heart in San Francisco."

Determinedly she began to clip at the sutures that bound the fresh scar in the man's chest. "Our medical technology has reached the point where organ transplants are now a viable option for numerous conditions—heart, liver, kidney disease, even some forms of blindness. The problem is there aren't nearly enough organs to go around. People are put on waiting lists, and if they're not lucky, it's the wait that kills them. For a while now, the medical ethicists have been warning us about the possibility of a black market for body parts developing here. They already exist in other countries."

"Scully, even if you're right, it doesn't figure," Mulder said. "There's no long-term business sense in dying. And what connection does this have to the crematorium deaths?"

"I don't know yet," Scully answered. "But I can tell you this much: The only thing that wasn't burned to a delicate crisp on Johnny Lo was his glass eye."

Curious to see if her theory was right, to see if the victim's heart had been removed, Scully returned to the task before her—snipping open the stitches on his chest.

She stepped back in alarm as just beneath the sutures the dead man's chest began to rise and fall. It was as if something were still pulsing inside. As if he were breathing.

It's impossible, Scully told herself.

"Oh, my God," she murmured. As she watched, the angry red wound opened—and a tiny green frog pulled itself out from beneath the skin and onto the dead man's chest.

"Talk about a frog in your throat," Mulder commented.

Once again the smoky gaming room was crowded and noisy. The din grew louder as the larger of the two jade vases was passed up to the table at the front of the room.

As before, the two men sat behind the teak table that held the carved wooden box filled with money.

The man called Tam carried the larger vase to the table. Lau adjusted his glasses and got to his feet. He reached into the larger vase and removed one of the name tiles.

"Hsin Shuyang!" he called.

The room abruptly fell silent. Hsin stared at the money box, his nerves warring between excitement and terror. He had been playing the game for months now. Finally it was his chance. The chance to win enough money to save Kim. And if he *didn't* win the money . . . no, he wouldn't even let himself think about that.

Lau held up the small jade vase and the white tile—the tile that could save Kim's life. Hsin felt his hopes rise as Lau dropped the white tile into the vase.

Tam carried the small vase through the crowd. He seemed to be moving unusually quickly. Everything was suddenly happening too fast. Hsin felt a bead of sweat drop between his shoulder blades as Tam set the vase in his hands. Some part of him couldn't believe this was real. Another part of him knew that two lives—Kim's and his own—depended on what happened in the next moments.

Hsin barely heard the shouts of encouragement from the men around him. He held the jade vase high overhead and shook it three times. There was a dragon carved on its side, he realized, a good-luck symbol. He hesitated only a moment, then closed his eyes, reached in, and removed a tile.

Hsin couldn't bear to look. Time seemed to slow to a dead stop. He kept his eyes closed, hoping, praying that the tile he held in his clenched fist was the white one. Around him he heard the others, impatient to know what he'd drawn. Hsin felt as if he couldn't move. Couldn't breathe. Hope and fear twisted together and formed a knot in the center of his chest. One way or the other, the tile would change his entire life.

He felt someone prying his fist open. *Let it*

be a white tile, he prayed. *Let me win the money for Kim.*

He opened his eyes as Tam held up the red tile and announced his fate to the room.

"*Yenjing!*" he called out.

The room erupted in more shouts. Hsin felt his legs shaking violently. He didn't think he could walk.

Then suddenly everything was moving fast again. He was helped up from his seat and escorted through the single doorway where Oi-Huan Li had last been seen.

Chapter Eight

Detective Glen Chao was at his desk the next morning, talking on the phone, when a covered glass jar was set on his desk. The jar held a small, live green frog.

Chao, puzzled, glanced up to see Scully and Mulder staring down at him.

Chao finished his conversation quickly, then hung up. "What's this?" he asked, picking up the jar.

"We're hoping you can tell us," Scully said in a hard voice. "It was found in the chest cavity of the man who was dumped in the grave."

"This?" Chao asked, pointing to the frog.

"You said the frog was a symbol of luck and prosperity," Scully reminded him. "Unless this is somebody's sick joke, I'd say it must have another meaning."

Chao shook his head and set the jar down. "Well, if it does, I don't know what it is. I mean, it could be some kind of . . . triad symbol. Something to do with organized crime . . . "

"Well, maybe you can tell me this," Scully went on. "Have you heard any word on the street about a black-market selling of body parts?"

"What? Here, in Chinatown?" the detective asked, his voice filled with disbelief.

"This man with the frog in his chest was missing a cornea and a kidney," Scully said, wanting to be sure he understood her. "They were taken *prior* to the time of death. *Before the final removal of his heart.* And I found residue of sterile ice on the skin in and around the incision in his chest. It is a substance that is used to preserve human organs for transplant."

Chao shook his head and laughed helplessly, as if what Scully was telling him were absurd. "I've never heard of such a thing," he said.

Mulder had been standing at the police

station window, intently watching their exchange, and watching Chao grow more and more uneasy by the second.

"We're going to need more help from you than that, Detective," Mulder said.

Chao's smile faded. "The implication being that I'm not trying to help?"

"No," Mulder said, stepping toward him.

Scully had no patience for wasting time with diplomacy. She said flatly, "My impression is that you either resent us being here or you feel some kind of protectiveness toward the Chinese community."

"Look, you don't even know what the hell you're dealing with," Chao said in a soft, angry voice. "This isn't some . . . pretty little lacquer box you can just take the lid off of and find out what's inside. You might see the face of a Chinese man here, but let me tell you something—the people on the streets don't see the same face. They see the face of a cop. American-born Chinese, ABC. To them, I'm just as white as you are."

Indignantly he stood up and reached for

his jacket, stopping to take a slip of white paper from his desk. "You think that because I speak the language, I can get all your answers for you. Tell me, what good is an interpreter when everyone speaks the language of silence?"

Chao slapped the piece of white paper against Mulder's coat as he walked past him.

"What's this?" Mulder asked.

"That's the name of the company that installed the carpet in Johnny Lo's apartment," Chao answered angrily. "I just happened to run across it while I was sitting here twiddling my thumbs. You coming with me or not?"

Chapter Nine

Twenty minutes later Chao, Mulder, and Scully stood in the dingy, dimly lit hallway of a Chinatown apartment building. Chao pressed a buzzer. On the other side of the door, they heard shuffling footsteps, then the sound of a dead bolt being unlocked.

The door opened a crack, and a man peered out over the safety chain. They could see only part of his face—that of a middle-aged man with a guarded expression.

"Mr. Hsin?" Chao held up his badge. "I'm Detective Chao with the San Francisco Police. Could we have a word with you?"

"I'm late for work," Hsin replied. He spoke in the slow, careful English of someone who was not yet comfortable with the language.

"It'll only take a minute," Chao assured him. "Could we come in, please?"

Hsin hesitated for a moment, then reluctantly unlatched the safety chain and let them in.

As they stepped into the apartment, Hsin closed the door and the agents finally got a good look at him. He was a slender, slightly stooped man in his late forties. His black hair was graying, and he wore a neatly pressed short-sleeved shirt and pants. But the most striking thing about him was the thick white bandage that covered one eye.

Scully spoke up at once. "Mr. Hsin, can I ask what happened to your eye?"

"An accident at work," Hsin answered stiffly. "Carpet tack."

Mulder and Scully exchanged a look of disbelief.

"How long have you lived in this country, Mr. Hsin?" Mulder asked.

"Three years," Hsin answered.

"Do you live here alone?" Mulder asked.

Before Hsin could answer, a young woman's voice called out from the next room, "Is someone there?"

Hsin pointed toward the bedroom. "My daughter," he explained to the three officers.

Curious, Chao walked toward the girl's room.

Scully began her line of questioning. "Mr. Hsin, you laid a carpet in an apartment that was occupied by a man named Johnny Lo."

Mulder moved into the kitchen, doing a visual survey of the apartment. He noted the Bay Area Carpeteers jacket hanging on a hook; the long white gauze curtains covering the venetian blinds; the neatly arranged ceramic tea set. It was clear that Hsin didn't have a lot of money, and yet he was trying to make a good home here.

Hsin looked confused by Scully's question about Johnny Lo. "I don't know the name," he said slowly. "The man I work for tells me the address only."

"Well, we contacted the man you work

for," Scully said. "He said this must have been a job you took on the side. He has no record of the work order."

Something caught Mulder's eye. On top of a wooden cabinet he saw a blue-and-white porcelain box and a round box carved of red cinnabar. Between them was a small red triangular tile.

Mulder picked up the tile and turned it over. On one side, a Chinese character was painted in gold.

Hsin seemed confused by Scully's questions. "What was the name of the man who lived in this apartment?" he asked her.

"His name was Johnny Lo," Scully repeated. She couldn't tell whether Hsin was genuinely having trouble understanding her or whether he was faking it.

"He's dead now. Murdered," Scully said, wanting to impress Hsin with the seriousness of the case. "And we think the carpet was laid there to cover up the evidence of his murder."

Hsin raised his eyebrows, looking surprised.

xxx

Detective Chao poked his head into the back bedroom. He saw framed Chinese prints on the walls, flowered curtains covering the windows. And a young woman lying in the bed, her eyes closed. She seemed feverish, frail. She had a look he'd seen before—of someone who was not entirely in this world, someone hovering between life and death.

Sensing his presence, she opened her eyes and sat up a little.

She spoke to him in Cantonese: "Where's my father?"

"He's here," Chao said in a reassuring voice.

"Who are you?" she asked.

She was pretty, Chao realized, and frightened. "I'm just here asking him some questions," he told her.

Seeing the troubled look on her face, he slipped away before she could ask anything more.

Scully held her notepad in front of her. So far she hadn't written a single thing on it. Hsin was still either confused by her questions or lying through his teeth. Her patience was already worn thin and eroding further by the second. Still, she pressed on. "Do you remember who called you about the job? Who asked you to do the work?"

"I think I remember this job," Hsin answered. "A man came to me, offered me cash."

"Did you see any bloodstains when you laid the carpet?" Scully asked.

"Bloodstains?" Hsin responded, shaking his head.

Detective Chao and Mulder returned to the kitchen at the same time. Mulder drew Scully's attention, gesturing to the door.

"Thank you, Mr. Hsin," Mulder said, ending the pointless interview. "If we need you, we'll get back to you, okay?"

Hsin smiled, looking relieved, and nodded.

Mulder and Scully left the apartment, but Detective Chao hung back, speaking to Hsin in Chinese.

"What's up?" Scully asked her partner.

"Tell you in a second," Mulder said. He was looking back through the open door of the apartment, his gaze focused on the two men. He watched as they talked, Hsin giving Chao a slight but deferential bow.

Scully watched with her arms folded. She didn't have a clue as to what they were saying, but Hsin seemed completely different with Chao, patting him on the shoulder almost as if he was trying to reassure him. Or—another possibility occurred to her—as if he knew him.

Seconds later the conversation ended and Chao walked into the hall, Hsin shutting the door behind him.

"What was that all about?" Mulder asked Chao.

"He's got the back window blocked up," Chao answered. "I told him it was a firetrap."

Mulder nodded, then held up the triangular red tile he'd found in Hsin's apartment.

"Do you know what this is?" Mulder asked.

Chao took it and studied it. "No."

"Do you know what it says?"

"It's the character for *wood*," Chao replied.

"*Wood?*" Mulder echoed.

"Yeah, why? What are you thinking?" Chao asked.

"That this guy didn't have an accident at work," Scully supplied.

"I think he's missing his eye," Mulder said. "And I'd like to know how he lost it."

"Maybe we should monitor Mr. Hsin's every movement," Scully suggested.

"Yeah," Mulder agreed. "And somehow I'm willing to bet he's not going to visit an ophthalmologist."

Chapter Ten

Hsin let out a sigh of relief as he closed the door behind his three visitors. But he pressed his ear against the door, trying to pick up what he could of their conversation. He could hear the woman speak. Did she believe him?

He turned at the sound of his daughter's soft voice. "Father?"

She was standing in her nightgown in the doorway that led to the bedrooms.

"Are you in some kind of trouble?" she asked in a worried voice.

"What are you doing?" Hsin demanded, alarmed to see her up. "Go right back to bed—you should be lying down! Now!"

She was definitely worse. She looked so pale, she was almost ghostly. He moved toward her, determined to send her back to bed, but she refused to budge.

"What happened to your eye?" she asked.

"Nothing, I had an accident," he told her gruffly.

"What kind of accident?"

"A work accident, that's all."

"You couldn't have," Kim said. Her body might be failing, but her mind was as sharp as ever. Her father was in danger, and she wasn't going to pretend that she didn't know it. "Last night when you got off work, nothing was wrong. You hurt it after—"

He turned back to face her. "It's no business of yours. Do you understand?"

"No, I don't understand," Kim replied, her voice soft but determined. *As stubborn as her mother had once been,* Hsin thought. Years ago in China, Hsin had watched his wife die of cancer. He couldn't bear to lose his daughter too.

"How will you get well?" he asked her, a note of desperation in his voice. "How will you get well if we don't have the money for the doctors?"

"What would I do if something happened to you?" she countered. Her voice softened. "I'm just worried about you—"

"I wake up every day and worry!" Hsin broke in. The fears he'd wrestled with for months, had carefully kept from her, poured out of him in an anguished voice. "Have I made a mistake? Am I being foolish? Have I made a mistake in coming to this country? Do our ancestors scorn us for leaving our home? Is that why you're sick now?"

"You're not to blame," Kim told him. She reached out a hand tentatively, then embraced him.

"Who *is* to blame?" he asked, his voice shaking. "If you can't get help, then who's to blame if not me?"

Hsin held his daughter in his arms. Tears streamed from under his eye patch, flowing red onto Kim's white nightgown.

It was after eight that night when Chao's car pulled up in front of his two-story town house in San Francisco's Richmond area. Chao had saved for five years to buy this place. Even now, every cent he made went into it. He'd just had the outside repainted and skylights installed in the kitchen and bedroom. San Francisco real estate was exorbitant and the town house was more than he could easily afford, but it was worth it. After years in the cramped Chinatown apartment where he'd grown up, the town house was Chao's proof that he'd made it. He'd never had any regrets. He was reminded of his success every time he came home to the spacious, high-ceilinged rooms with their polished oak floors.

Now he cut the car engine and his headlights blinked off. He got out and started up the walk. His gait quickened as he saw something on the front door.

The pristine white paint was covered with ragged, bright-red characters. *Tsang fang.* Haunted house. The same characters he'd found on Johnny Lo's door.

Nervously Chao touched the paint. It was fresh, wet, still runny. He glanced around, wondering if the culprits were in sight. But there was no movement on the street, no sign of anyone.

Chao fumbled as he put his keys in the door. He swore silently. His hands were shaking.

He inched the door open. For a long moment, he stood perfectly still. He didn't sense anything out of the ordinary. He could hear the refrigerator humming in the kitchen, the clock ticking on the living room mantel, his own heart pounding. No one was here. It was just him.

Moving silently, he closed the door behind him and slid on the safety chain.

He turned on the hallway light. It shed just enough light into the living room for Chao to see that the town house wasn't empty after all. He had visitors. Three masked demons, their faces appearing out of the darkness, almost as if they were disembodied. As if they were ghosts.

Chao felt a wave of pure terror wash through him. This time, they'd come for him.

Chapter Eleven

Nighttime in Chinatown was never truly dark. There were always neon lights, headlights, streetlights, the lights of TV screens seen through apartment windows, and the lights of the few stores and restaurants that stayed open all night long.

Outside Hsin's building, a pack of firecrackers exploded. The youthful perpetrators tore off down the alley, unaware of the nondescript rental car that was parked there. The car where Mulder sat, waiting.

Mulder checked his watch and looked up at Hsin's building. He could see lights in Hsin's apartment. The curtains were drawn. So far, following Shuyang Hsin had gotten them exactly nowhere. Ever since they'd begun watching the apartment, Hsin had stayed inside.

Mulder rubbed his eyes, then leaned his head back. He straightened like a shot when a hand yanked open the passenger door.

"You look like you just saw a ghost," Scully said, sliding into the passenger seat and shutting the door.

"I'm getting a little tired," Mulder admitted. "And jumpy. One more string of firecrackers goes off, and I'm going to get out of the car and shoot somebody."

Scully looked up at the lit window. "He hasn't left his apartment, has he?"

"No," Mulder answered. "I'm glad you're here. I was just about to go up and ask Mr. Hsin if I could use his bathroom."

"Well, you can use the one down at St. Francis Hospital," Scully said, fastening her seat belt.

"What do you mean?"

"Detective Chao was attacked in his town house tonight. I just talked to Lieutenant Neary. He says he's cut up pretty bad."

"Well, who cut him?" Mulder asked.

"I don't know," Scully said. "But I think we should go check it out."

As Mulder and Scully set off for the hospital, a man walked toward Hsin's building. A man with graying hair and a hard expression in his eyes. The same man who had come for Oi-Huan Li just before he lost consciousness for the last time.

Hsin was sitting at the kitchen table, eating dinner, when he heard the door buzzer.

"Who is it?" he called through the closed door.

"You know who it is," a man's voice replied.

Hsin recognized the voice. It was the doctor, the man who ran the game. He never appeared in the gaming room, but everyone knew he controlled it.

A sick feeling went through Hsin as he realized something else. The other night, after he'd been given the tea to drink, everything had become hazy. It was hard to remember exactly what had happened. But he was fairly certain it had been the doctor who had held the scalpel. The doctor who had taken his eye.

Years ago, the doctor had come to this country speaking no English. Even though he'd gotten a medical degree in China, he was unable to find work. He'd played the game and had won hundreds of thousands of dollars. It had made him a rich man.

Hsin hesitated a moment, then opened the door.

The doctor wasted no time on pleasantries. "I did not receive your payment," he said.

Hsin thought of his last conversation with Kim, and he knew what he had to say. "I want out."

"You want out of the game?" Unconcerned by this announcement, the doctor pulled a plum from his pocket and began to eat it.

"I quit," Hsin told him, nervous but determined. "No more."

"You've been luckier than most," the doctor said. "All this time and only one bad draw. Most men would be happy to trade places with you. The pot is now almost two million dollars. One draw, Mr. Hsin. One draw and maybe you'll win more than I did."

"But maybe I'm not so lucky," Hsin protested.

"The money could help to save your daughter's life," the man reminded him.

"Maybe I'm not so lucky," Hsin repeated, finally speaking his fears aloud. "Maybe my daughter will die with no father at her side. Alone with strangers."

"You should have thought of this before you entered the game, Hsin. You have to keep playing. You know the rules. No one talks about the game . . . no one leaves the game."

Kim heard the voices in the kitchen. Curious, she got out of bed and listened at the door. She didn't recognize the visitor's voice. It was definitely not the handsome young man who'd looked in on her the day before. Who was this strange man arguing with her father?

"But my daughter!" Hsin insisted.

"Those are the rules," the doctor told him

coldly. "They cannot be broken, or it's said the fires of *Ti Yu* will consume you."

Hsin was pleading now, hands clasped in front of him. "Please! I beg you!"

"It is not my choice," the doctor said. He opened the door and left, leaving Hsin suffering in the prison of his dilemma.

Behind the door, Kim held her hand over her mouth, fighting the temptation to tell her father that she had overheard. She didn't know who the stranger was, what he'd been talking about, or what her father wanted to get out of. Only one thing was clear. Her father's life was in as much danger as her own.

Chapter Twelve

Mulder and Scully passed through a set of double doors that led to the wing where Glen Chao had been assigned a room. Lieutenant Neary was standing at the end of the hall, talking to a couple of uniformed officers. He broke off his conversation as he caught sight of the two FBI agents.

"How is he?" Scully asked.

"He's gone," Neary said tensely. "When I got down here to see him, he wasn't in his bed."

"Did anybody see him leave?" Mulder asked.

"Well, the nurse said they'd just finished sewing him up and he got up to go to the bathroom, and that's the last anybody saw of him."

"Why would he just take off?" Scully wondered aloud.

Neary shook his head, mystified.

"Can I see his chart?" Mulder asked.

"His chart?" Neary repeated, surprised. "Sure, I guess."

Scully wondered where Mulder was going with this. As Neary headed off to request Chao's chart, she questioned her partner: "You want to see what his injuries were?"

"No," Mulder replied. "I want to see what his blood type is."

"His blood type?"

"Why would he run, Scully?" Mulder asked.

"You think Chao's involved?" Scully responded.

"Maybe all his heel dragging was a diversion and the ghost stories a ruse," Mulder said. "What was the hemotype of the blood we found on the carpet padding?"

Scully pulled out her notepad and flipped through it as Neary returned with the chart.

"O negative," Scully said. It was one of the rarer blood types.

Mulder took the medical chart from Neary, then read aloud, "'Glen Chao. O negative.'" He handed Scully the chart and turned to Neary, saying, "Well, that's a coincidence."

"Now, wait a minute," Neary said. "What do you mean?"

"That the blood we found on the carpet padding in the victim's apartment was Detective Chao's," Scully said.

"And I'd be willing to bet that he's the one who ordered the new carpet installed," Mulder added.

Scully looked up from the chart, realizing the implication of Mulder's words. "Mr. Hsin," she said.

Mulder nodded. "Yeah, I don't think that conversation they had was about any firetrap."

Fifteen minutes later Mulder and Scully stood in the hallway outside Hsin's apartment, waiting for him to answer their knock.

The door opened slowly. This time it was not Hsin but his daughter who stared out at the agents. She was wearing a white bathrobe, and there were red, puffy circles under her eyes. "Yes?" the girl said apprehensively.

"Hi," Scully began. "We're looking for Mr. Hsin. Is he home?"

"No. I'm sorry."

Mulder and Scully exchanged a brief glance. Neither of them could believe it. They'd watched Hsin's apartment all day, and all day he'd stayed inside. As soon as they'd broken their watch, he'd gone.

"Are you his daughter?" Scully asked, unwilling to give up.

"Yes," the girl answered. "My name is Kim."

"May we talk to you?" Scully asked.

Kim looked at them hesitantly, then closed the door and unhooked the safety chain.

Mulder and Scully followed the young woman into the living room, where she sat in a chair. Scully watched the girl with concern. She had the distinct impression that Kim was sitting because it was simply too much of an effort for her to stand.

"What's your father involved in, Kim?" Mulder asked.

Kim didn't answer at first. "I don't know," she said at last. "Yesterday a strange man visited him. And he goes out a lot. I know he does it for me. *Because* of me."

"You're sick, aren't you?" Scully said, her voice sympathetic.

"I was diagnosed with acute lymphocytic leukemia six months ago," the girl said.

"But that's a treatable form of cancer," Scully said. "It's commonly cured with bone marrow transplants."

"But first they would have to give me chemotherapy," Kim said. "We have no money or insurance. We can't afford those treatments. Now I fear that my father may have done something illegal. That he's made a mistake and something bad is coming."

Scully had no answer for that. She knew that as advanced as American medical care was, it was often limited to those who could afford it. Hospitalization usually started at about $1,400 a day, and that was just for the bed. Chemotherapy; the process of finding a proper donor; harvesting and then transplanting the donor's bone marrow into Kim—all that could run into hundreds of thousands of dollars. The situation was complicated by the fact that there was an acute shortage of matching donors for minorities, simply because the donor pools were smaller. Without insurance or substantial savings, the kind of medical care that Kim needed was impossible. Even if her father could pay for insurance, few insurance companies would take on someone with preexisting acute lymphocytic leukemia. And of course, if Hsin was in the country illegally, the situation was much worse. Then Kim wouldn't even be able to get onto the donor lists.

"Who is this man who came to visit your father?" Mulder asked.

"I don't know him," Kim said. "I just know that my father said he wants out—he wants out. But of what I don't know."

I'll bet it's something that explains why he's wearing a bandage over his eye, Scully thought.

Mulder reached into his pocket and pulled out the triangular red tile he'd found the last time he was in the Hsins' apartment.

"Do you know what this is, Kim?" Mulder asked.

Kim took the tile and examined it. "No."

"It was sitting here on the cabinet before. Do you know what it says?"

"It's the symbol for *wood*," Kim said, confirming what Chao had told them. "And in Chinese medicine it also corresponds to the eyes. Like fire corresponds to the heart, and earth to the flesh."

She handed the tile back to Mulder.

Mulder glanced at Scully. This was all starting to add up in a way he didn't like.

Scully picked up a sheet of paper on the end table beside her. Her pulse quickened as she recognized a familiar array of abbreviations and symbols. "This is a human leukocyte workup," she said, showing Kim the paper. "Was your father rejected as a bone marrow donor?"

"Yes," the girl said. "Several months ago. They said that if he donated his marrow, either my body would reject it, or his cells would attack my body and cause liver disease."

Scully continued to scan the report, wondering how much Hsin had not told his daughter. Then she noticed something she hadn't picked up on at first: the date at the top of the page. "This report is from the Organ Procurement Organization," she said. "It's dated only a month ago. Your father had an HLA, but he also had his kidneys measured, and his liver . . . "

Mulder listened, feeling a familiar sense of excitement as the pieces of the case finally started to come together. Hsin's visit to the Organ Procurement Organization had nothing to do with giving Kim his own bone marrow. No, the organs listed were meant for someone—or something—else. Something connected to Johnny Lo's glass eye and the corpse they'd found in the cemetery.

Mulder turned over the smooth red tile,

adding in what Kim had just told them. And finally understanding.

A chill went through him as he said, "They're playing some kind of game."

Chapter Thirteen

Hsin felt a growing dread as he entered the gaming room. He'd always understood the risks intellectually, but it wasn't until last time that the risks had become real. Had become *his*. Not too long ago, he'd felt hope when he entered this room. Now he felt like a man walking to his own execution.

As always, smoke filled the air, and the gaming room was buzzing with voices.

Hsin made his way through the crowd to a chair and took a deep breath, trying to calm his racing heart. He looked apprehensively at the head table, where the gray-bearded man was unlocking the carved wooden box.

Sweat beading his brow, Hsin stared at the stacks of hundred-dollar bills, as if by staring hard enough, he could will them to be his. *The game is worth it,* he told himself. *All I need is one lucky draw, and Kim will be healed and our problems will be over.*

There was no one in the stark white hallway of the Organ Procurement Organization in downtown San Francisco. It was well past normal business hours, and the outer office was dark and deserted.

"Looks like they've all gone home," Mulder said.

"No," Scully said, "there should be someone here round the clock, monitoring the phones and computers. Time is critical in transplants. An organization like this has to be able to instantly notify hospitals as soon as organs become available."

Scully pounded on the glass door, noting that the lettering there was both English and Chinese.

Finally a woman staffer with long brown hair stepped out of the back office to see who was raising such a fuss. She came toward the glass door and reluctantly opened it a crack.

"Agents Mulder and Scully," Scully said, holding up her badge.

"Thanks," Scully said as she and Mulder stepped inside. "We need some information, and we need it as soon as possible."

"What kind of information? the woman asked.

"You had a man come here named Shuyang Hsin. He had an HLA workup and some other—"

"I think I may know what this is about," the woman broke in.

"What?" Mulder asked.

"Well, we've seen a number of Asian men come in for typing and antigen workups, but when we find a compatible recipient for them, their doctor says that they've left the area or disappeared."

"Do you have a name or phone number for this doctor?" Mulder asked.

Hsin held his breath as he dropped the tile bearing his name into the large jade jar. Tam, the youngest of the three men, continued to circulate the jar through the room, making sure that no one avoided putting in his name. Then slowly, almost ceremoniously, he carried the jar back to the table at the front of the room.

Lau, the man with the wire-rimmed glasses, got to his feet.

Slowly he dipped his hand into the large vase and pulled out a tile. He held it up to read the name.

It can't happen again, Hsin told himself. *It's against the odds to be chosen twice.*

A wave of sickness rolled through him as the man read aloud, "*Hsin Shuyang!*"

It was impossible! How could he be drawn again?

Hsin watched, frozen, as the smaller vase was passed from hand to hand, steadily making its way toward him. Everything depended on this draw. He fixed his eyes on the box of money. Everything.

Mulder was at the wheel of the rental car as it peeled out of the parking lot of the Organ

Procurement Organization. He turned onto one of San Francisco's narrow streets. For once, there was no traffic. He floored the accelerator, hoping they weren't already too late.

Beside him, Scully listened intently on her cell phone. "Yes, thank you," she said into the receiver. She turned to Mulder. "The phone company's giving me an address for the doctor's phone number," she told him. She turned her attention back to the phone. "Three-one-one Washington," she said. "Right. Thank you."

Mulder parked in front of a restaurant with a small red pagoda over the front door. The sign on the door said CLOSED. The restaurant was dark inside. Neon lights above the door bathed the building in a deep red glow. Mulder stared at the building, puzzled. It shouldn't have been a restaurant at all.

"Three eleven Washington, right?" he asked Scully.

"Yeah," Scully said, sounding equally surprised. "That's where this doctor's phone is registered."

"Some clinic," Mulder murmured. His eyes narrowed as a familiar, slightly built man approached. "Hey, Scully, look who's here."

Glen Chao walked up to the closed restaurant, nonchalantly checked the street around him, then unlocked the door and entered the building.

Mulder smiled. "This must be the place after all."

Hsin held the small jade vase high overhead and tried to stop his hands from trembling. He looked again at the dragon carved on one side of the vase and hoped it would bring him luck.

The crowd around him was boisterous as he shook the vase once, twice, three times. And then they quieted, waiting for Hsin to choose a tile.

Hsin prayed for good fortune, then he dipped his hand into the vase and closed it around a smooth wooden triangle.

He didn't look at the tile he'd drawn but kept it grasped tightly in his fist.

Tam walked over to Hsin and grabbed his clenched hand. His fist was pried open and the triangular tile removed.

Still Hsin couldn't bear to look.

Then he heard Tam announce in a loud voice, *"Xin!"*

The room erupted at the word. Hsin backed away, tried to run, but a human wall surrounded him. Closed in on him. He was caught like a hare trapped by hunters.

Tam grabbed Hsin roughly and began pulling him toward the front of the room. "You know the rules," he said.

Hsin closed his one good eye. *Yes, I know the rules,* he answered silently. *And now I will die for them.*

All eyes followed as Shuyang Hsin was led to the front of the room. No one noticed the young Chinese man as he slipped in the back. Silently, Chao watched as Hsin was dragged from sight—to pay the price for his unlucky draw.

Chapter Fourteen

Mulder tried the restaurant door that Chao had gone through. "Another locked door," he murmured to Scully.

"You're not telling me you want to give up now and go home?" she asked warily.

"No," Mulder said, reaching into an inner pocket and pulling out a thin metal tool.

Trying to look as if she were casually standing on the street, Scully shielded Mulder from passersby as he worked the pick.

Seconds later the lock clicked open. Inside, everything was quiet, the dining room dark and deserted. The only light came from the red neon outside. Chinese characters painted on the restaurant's windows cast long reddish shadows across the floor.

For a moment Mulder stood perfectly still,

letting his eyes adjust to the darkness. He could make out overturned chairs stacked on top of tables. Glasses, silverware, and folded cloth napkins on metal carts. There was no sign of Glen Chao.

Convinced that Chao was not in the room, the two agents switched on their flashlights and moved deeper into the darkened room. Where had Chao gone? Mulder wondered. And why would a doctor be working from a restaurant?

They moved silently from the dining room into the kitchen. Scully's light reflected on stainless steel counters, industrial stoves and sinks, stacks of pots, pans, and woks, and utensils hanging from hooks.

Mulder stopped, sniffing the air. "That's definitely not Chinese food I'm smelling," he said.

Scully moved up behind him, training her beam on the ground at their feet—and a thin stream of liquid that had pooled on the red tile floor.

Mulder stooped down and touched a finger to the liquid.

"It smells like rubbing alcohol," he said.

"Or sterile ice," Scully suggested.

The source of the liquid, Mulder saw, was a large stainless steel freezer. The metal gleamed as Mulder's light passed over it.

Moving quickly, Mulder began to search the freezer. He pulled out package after package of frozen food: egg rolls, chicken breasts, sauces, soups . . .

Scully was beginning to wonder if the search was useless when he asked, "Scully, what's this?"

His light illuminated a clear rectangular plastic container filled with ice.

Mulder took the plastic container out of the freezer and opened it. Buried in the ice was a small, round glass jar. Mulder wiped away the frost so that he could see what was inside it. A sick feeling went through him when he realized what he held, but he knew without a doubt that they were in the right place.

Inside the glass jar, a frozen human eyeball stared back at him.

Hsin sat in the hard-backed chair. The same chair he'd sat in just before he lost his eye. The same chair Li had sat in before he lost his life.

Hsin had drunk the tea that was offered to him. His trembling had stopped. He was no longer conscious when the doctor held his eyelid open and peered at his one remaining pupil.

The doctor gestured to his assistant, a man dressed like him in light green surgical scrubs and latex gloves. Together they lifted Hsin's limp body from the chair and carried him to the operating table . . .

The game was over for the night, the gaming room gradually emptying out. Mr. Lau carried the small jade vase back toward the table. He stopped as Glen Chao closed a hand over his wrist.

Lau set the vase on the table, then turned to confront Chao. "What are you doing here?" he asked angrily.

"I can't let you do this," Chao answered.

Lau stared pointedly at the detective's bandage. "You've been warned once, Chao," he said. "There will be no more warnings."

This time Chao refused to let himself be frightened off. "Let Hsin go," he said. "His daughter is dying. You'll be killing two people, not one."

"That is the game, Mr. Chao. Those are the risks. And you're just as much a part of it as I am. We've paid you well to protect the game from the foreigners."

Chao nodded, as if acknowledging the truth of Lau's words. "Then this game," he said quietly, and unexpectedly his voice rose to a shout, *"is over!"*

Before anyone could stop him, Chao reached for the table where the vases and money box sat. In one quick, powerful movement, he grabbed the edge of the table and wrenched it onto its side, sending the wooden box and jade vases flying. The money box splintered as it hit the floor, scattering hundred-dollar bills. The two jade vases smashed into jagged green shards.

Chao grasped the legs of the table, looking at what he had done. His eyes were riveted on the remains of the smaller vase. Among the broken fragments of jade were dozens of red tiles. They were *all* red tiles. There wasn't a single white one.

"They're all the same," Chao said, stunned. For the first time he truly understood that the lottery was more than dangerous. It was evil. He raised his voice to a shout. *"The game is fixed!"*

His words had an immediate effect. The players who remained in the room pushed forward to see the proof for themselves. Night after night they'd sat in this room, captives of desperation and fear. Now a wave of rage swept through the gaming room, catching everyone in its fury.

"It was all a lie!" shouted one man.

"This game has no winners!" cried another.

The room erupted into chaos as the players took charge. A group of men rushed toward the overturned teak table and scrambled after the money on the floor. Others had no interest in the money. All they wanted was revenge. They smashed tables and chairs, making weapons out of the broken pieces. Then they closed in on Lau and Wong.

In the darkened kitchen Mulder and Scully froze. They could hear noises—angry voices and what sounded like furniture hitting the floor.

"What is that?" Scully asked.

"I don't know," Mulder said, "but it's coming from upstairs."

Hsin lay stretched out on the makeshift operating table, his arms and legs held down by thick leather straps. His shirt and undershirt had been stripped from his body. He was breathing with the light, shallow breaths of the unconscious.

Scully shined her light toward the back of the kitchen. "This way," she said, seeing a door with an Exit sign over it.

The two agents rushed up the darkened

stairway, their guns drawn. The noise increased in volume as they neared the second floor.

Mulder pushed open the red door to the gaming room, then stood transfixed. It was as though he and Scully had just stepped into the middle of a riot—only he had no idea who was fighting or why. Men were shouting, pushing. Others were trying to flee as quickly as possible. In the center of the frenzy, a middle-aged man with wire-rimmed glasses and another with a gray beard were cowering under a steady rain of blows.

Wordlessly, Mulder and Scully watched the scene unfolding around them. As his eyes scanned the crowd, Mulder spotted a man making his way out a door in the back. A man he recognized as Chao.

Chapter Fifteen

Hsin moved slowly through the murky water. He was miles and miles below an endless, dark sea. He was trying to swim to the surface. But it was easier to let the water take him, to float in the warm, heavy currents, to spiral down into the depths. His body felt heavy. Every movement was slow, achingly difficult. Yet somehow he knew that it was important to reach the surface. There was something there that he had to see. And he knew that if he let himself be pulled into the depths of the sea, he'd never come up again.

In the makeshift operating room behind the gaming hall, a counter held an array of standard surgical supplies: scalpels, bandages, hypodermics, and a large container of sterile ice, awaiting organs. Also on the counter was something not quite standard: several glass containers, each holding a live frog.

Hsin lay on the operating table, a bright light shining down on him. The tea had done its work. He was perfectly still, unconscious, as the doctor's assistant used a surgical swab to apply orange Betadyne solution to the skin on his chest.

The doctor ripped a length of surgical plastic from a spool and pressed it down against the unconscious man's chest. He never saw Hsin's remaining eye open.

Hsin had no idea how much time had passed before he reached the surface. He only knew that he had finally made his way through the murky water. The warm currents were stronger than ever. They were pulling at him, claiming him, and he knew he couldn't remain on the surface for long. Soon he would begin the long journey down. But now he took a breath of sweet, cool air and realized that the darkness belonged to the waters.

For just a moment he could see.

What he saw was the ghost of his daughter, Kim. She moved toward him, her eyes filled with grief. She didn't try to speak, but Hsin knew without a doubt that she was grieving for him. He wanted to comfort her as he had when she was a little girl. To hold her in his arms and tell her that everything would be all right.

Tears streamed down Hsin's cheek, but he could not find the strength to move.

Kim held out a hand to him and smiled, as if once again she wanted him to follow her.

He knew that was impossible. He would never follow her again. "Forgive me," he murmured to the vision. "I beg you to forgive me."

Then Hsin saw the doctor step forward from the darkness. He was gowned and masked, just like the doctors in the hospital where Kim had gone for tests.

Hsin struggled for another glimpse of his daughter. Where had she gone? Had she heard him?

"Forgive me," he said again.

The assistant handed the doctor a stainless steel scalpel.

The doctor's voice was hard and cynical as he replied to Hsin's desperate plea, "They forgive you." Holding the scalpel steady, he lowered it to Hsin's chest and began to slice through the orange-stained skin.

The doctor had barely begun his work when the door slammed open and Chao burst into the room, his revolver held in both hands.

"Step away," Chao ordered.

"You're too late," the doctor replied, continuing to cut.

"I said *step away!*" Chao shouted.

"Chao, don't be a fool," the doctor replied.

Chao didn't bother with another warning. He took aim and squeezed the trigger. The blast knocked the doctor off his feet. He fell backward, landing hard on the floor.

Suddenly, from behind Chao, Mulder's voice cut through the room. "Chao, hands in the air!" he ordered. "*Hands in the air!*"

Slowly Chao raised his hands, letting the gun fall to the floor.

Scully moved into the room, training her weapon on the doctor's assistant. She put a hand on Hsin's neck, searching for a pulse. Her fingertips felt a weak but steady beat in the carotid artery. "He's still alive," she said.

Mulder didn't waste time. He pushed Chao against the wall and cuffed him. Chao didn't seem concerned by the handcuffs. His attention was on the wounded man on the floor.

Mulder followed Chao's gaze. Although the doctor had been shot in the shoulder, he seemed disturbingly calm, staring up at Chao with a look of cold determination.

"You should have killed me," he said to Chao in Chinese.

Mulder looked from the doctor to Chao and asked, "What did he say?"

Chao looked shaken, like a man who knew he was doomed. His eyes never strayed from the doctor's as he answered Mulder with a translation that, although not literal, was accurate: "He said the game's not over."

Chapter Sixteen

At ten the next morning Scully stood in one of the San Francisco Police Department's interrogation rooms. The room was dimly lit, save for a light over the table in the center of the room, where the doctor, whose name was Yip, sat.

A sling braced the arm that had taken Chao's shot. Neither the injury nor the fact that he was in police custody seemed to faze Yip. He seemed entirely at ease, casually smoking a cigarette.

He spoke calmly, lyrically, as if narrating a documentary on Chinese folklore. "My people live with ghosts. The ghosts of our fathers— and our father's fathers."

Scully listened, unimpressed.

"They call to us from distant memory,"

he went on, "showing us the path."

Scully couldn't take any more of his act. "No ghosts called to those men," she told him. "*You* did, by preying on their hopelessness and their desperation."

"Yes, they were desperate," he admitted. "Just as I was desperate when I first came to this country—but I have committed no crime."

Scully's voice hardened. "You cheated those men out of life by promising them prosperity when the only possible reward was death."

"In my belief, death is nothing to be feared—it's merely a stage of transition. But life without hope—now, that's living Hell. So *hope* was my gift to these men." He registered Scully's scornful expression. "I don't expect you to understand."

"I understand this," Scully said. "You are going to prison for a very long time."

Just then, the door opened behind Yip, and Mulder poked his head into the room.

"Can I talk to you for a minute?" he asked Scully.

Scully gave Yip a final look, then followed Mulder into the hallway. She saw that Lieutenant Neary was with him.

Mulder closed the door behind them and turned to face Scully.

"I just got back from St. Francis Hospital," Mulder said. "Hsin's still in intensive care. He was given some sort of drug to knock him out; they're not sure what it is, but he's conscious again. They just want to watch him for a while."

"What about his daughter?" Scully asked.

"I checked with the Organ Procurement Organization," Mulder said. "She's been put on the donor recipient list."

"That's great," Scully said. Then, sensing that something remained unspoken, she asked, "What's wrong?"

Neary and Scully exchanged a look.

"It's our case against this guy," Neary said, nodding toward the interrogation room. "We've had our task force interviewing everybody we busted at the gaming parlor last night."

"And?" Scully asked.

"They've put up a wall of silence," Mulder said. "They all claim they were members of some social club, that they saw nothing."

"Well, what about Chao?" Scully asked, impatient with all the talk of ghosts. "His testimony alone would be enough to lock this guy up."

Neary stared at the ground. "We can't find him."

"Chao was supposed to testify before a grand jury this morning," Mulder explained. "When he didn't show up, the police went to his home. He's disappeared."

Chapter Seventeen

Glen Chao awoke to the sound of a switch being thrown. He became conscious slowly. He was lying flat on his back in some sort of narrow room, the walls close around him and the ceiling so low he couldn't sit up.

His head hurt and his brain felt foggy. He couldn't remember going to sleep. He didn't know where he was. Nothing seemed familiar.

Except the small blue pilot flame that he could see from the corner of his eye.

And then he heard a sound—a steady hissing sound of gas escaping dozens of tiny jets, followed by a sickening *pop* as each of the jets was lit—and he knew exactly where he was.

Inside the crematorium.

Already it was hot, unbearably hot. He

could feel and smell his hair and clothes start-ing to burn.

Chao did the only thing left for him to do.

He reached into his pocket and pulled out a set of keys. Desperately he used a key to scratch the surface of the oven roof—a last message for others to find—naming the ones responsible for his death.

It took only a second. Finished, Chao stared at his work with grim satisfaction. The same symbol Johnny Lo had scratched into another very similar oven.

Then a whooshing sound filled the cham-ber and a solid curtain of flame filled the crematorium.

Soon all that would be left of Detective Chao was a pile of ash. And on the ceiling of the oven, the Chinese symbol for *Ghost*.

THE
X-FILES

X MARKS THE SPOT

A novel by Les Martin
Based on the television series created by Chris Carter
Based on the teleplay written by Chris Carter

Class of the doomed...
The FBI thinks Agent Fox Mulder is strange – or worse. He keeps insisting that aliens are running amok on earth. His lovely and level-headed partner, Agent Dana Scully, is supposed to keep him in line. But that's hard to do when they're investigating an Oregon high school class full of corpses and the walking dead.

Yes, Mulder's theories about the class of '89 are beyond strange. But in a world where minds are turned off like lights, bodies blossom with otherworldly scars, and the night explodes with blinding evil, Fox Mulder may not be strange at all. He may just be the one with the answers nobody's ready to hear...

ISBN 0 00 675182 2

Don't miss the other X-Files novels by Les Martin:

X-Files #2: Darkness Falls   ISBN 0 00 675183 0
X-Files #3: Tiger, Tiger   ISBN 0 00 675184 9

THE
X-FILES

DARKNESS FALLS

A novel by Les Martin
Based on the television series created by Chris Carter
Based on the teleplay written by Chris Carter

Timberrrr!

FBI agents Fox Mulder and Dana Scully are tracking terror in the tall timber. And they've got their work cut out for them . . .

How can men hard as nails melt away into thin air?
Is it eco-warriors trying to protect their beloved forest?
Or an unearthly evil indulging in a feeding frenzy –
every night, when the light fails?

One things is certain: Scully and Mulder need answers
– before darkness falls . . . for good.

ISBN 0 00 675183 0

THE
X-FILES

GOBLINS

A novel by Charles Grant
Based on the television series created by Chris Carter.

Opening the X-Files...
Meet Mulder and Scully, FBI. The agency maverick
and the female agent assigned to keep him in line.
Their job: investigate the eeriest unsolved mysteries in
modern America, from pyro-psychics to death row
demonics, from rampaging Sasquatches to alien inva-
sions. The cases the Bureau want handled quietly, but
quickly, before the public finds out what's *really* out
there. And panics.
The cases filed under 'X'.

'*The X-Files* is a true masterpiece. There's no more
challenging series on television and, as a bonus, it's also
brainy fun.'   *Los Angeles Times*

ISBN 0 00 648204 X